1

Bibliografische Information der Deutschen Nationalbibliothek Die Deutsche Nationalbibliothek verzeichnet diese Publikation in der Deutschen Nationalbibliografie; detaillierte bibliografische Daten sind im Internet über http://dnb.d-nb.de abrufbar.

Revision 4

Print, Cover and Distribution by
Books on Demand GmbH, Norderstedt

All characters and events in this book are fictious.
Any resemblance to persons living or dead is concidential

A special thanks to Katraka
for helping me out with correcting the english

ISBN: 9783837016161

Elven Song and Angel's Glory

Written by
Alexandria Werder

For Mom, because I thought you'd love this as present.

Index

The Song of Eternity

here was once a soft song in the world. The song was a beautiful one, played by one whose beauty matched the song that he played. He never left the place he played at, because he was never disturbed there. There was a waterfall, and that waterfall fell in to the wide river, and the wide river flowed onward through the valley. Both sung with the song in harmony. There was a great wind, and the wind blew down the high cliffs, touching the trees, and the trees' leaves rustled softly with the wind passing. Both sung with the song in harmony. The player of the song had become part of the place, and had forgotten everything but the song he played eternally. There was nothing in this place but the song.

One day, a maiden heard the song. She thought it beautiful, and listened a long time. She wondered, after that long time, how one could play such a beautiful song, and wished to find the source. So she followed the melody, until she came upon a grand waterfall. She listened there, and she knew, the waterfall was an instrument, but it was not all of the song. She looked down the high cliffs, and saw a grand forest, separated by a wide river. Somewhere down there, she knew, were more parts of the song. So she looked for a way down, and she found a steep path leading to the forest.

Upon the cliff's wall, she heard the wind singing, and she knew, this too was part of the grand song that she heard. But the wind and the waterfall alone were not the song itself. They were instruments, making the song more beautiful than before. She continued to follow the path, reaching the ground of the forest, covered in leaves and flowers of all colors. She wondered if this, too, was part of the song, or if this beauty followed the song. She pondered no longer though, and stepped onward, hearing both waterfall and wind. At last, she reached the river. The river flowed, splashing in rhythm, as the leaves of the trees rustled along. Both were in harmony, and sung with the song. She knew, these, too, were instruments. She knelt by the river, taking a drink from the water more clear than even perfect glass, watching the colorful fish that had gathered. She smiled as some of them were as curious of her as she of them. But she left the riverside after a short while. She still wished to know where the rest of the song was. So she stepped away, back in to the forest. All she had was a sense she could barely grasp, the song echoing and ever-present.

Her steps led her onward through the forest. It was not long, and she stepped upon a clearing, light shining upon it as if it were a most sacred of places. In midst of the clearing was a young man, playing a harp. From his lips escaped words of clearest beauty, and so she knew, she had found what she had been seeking. She stepped upon the clearing, quietly, and sat below the young man, watching him, he embraced by roots and vines that claimed him as part of this forest, just as he had claimed the forest as part of his song.

She did not know how long she listened. It mattered nothing, though. All she knew was that she loved the song as much as the man. So she stood, stepping around him, and for the first time since she heard the song, she spoke, her voice so soft that it barely touched the song about. „Dearest One," she said,

„Why is your song so far from where it can be heard?" And for the first time since he had begun his song, he opened his eyes. For the first time, since he had begun to play, he looked about. And for the first time since he had come here, he paused his singing to speak. „Why is it that you came so near, when you can listen afar?"

She thought of his words, but could give little more answer than a word and a smile. „Curiosity." was what she had said, and she sat again by his feet, glancing up at him. „Sing, I beg you, Dearest One. I love you, and I love your song, and I will envy the Forest eternally for embracing you." He closed his eyes, and he sung. The forest sung with him, and she closed her eyes, and in thought, she sung too.

A long time passed, before she then decided what she loved more. She stood again, laying a soft hand on the young man's shoulder. „I will challenge the Forest." she said to him. Then she left, stepping to the river. She sung with the river, and as she sung, she tried to sing more clear than the splashing water. She sung so long with the river, until it silenced. She smiled, turning to the trees, and sung with the trees, trying to sing sweeter than the rustling leaves, and she sung so long until the trees silenced. She smiled, and looked up the cliffs.

She climbed the cliffs, but the winds were not an easy challenge. Upon the path to the forest, the winds blew loud and clear, and she had to sing louder and clearer than the wind. And she did so, until so much time passed that the winds stopped blowing. She smiled, despite being tired, and stepped on, until she was at the peak of the waterfall. There she looked down, hearing the thundering echoes of the waterfall's song, and she knew, she had to be louder and clearer than the waterfall. So she sang with all her heart, her voice echoing through the forest below, just as the song that gave life to all. And she sung so long until the waterfall ceased and was silent, leaving her alone to sing with the grand and beautiful song.

The Maiden, she wished now only sleep, but equally, she wished only to be near the one she loved. She climbed down in to the forest, then stepped again upon the clearing with the young man. The forest still embraced him tightly. She stepped toward him, softly touching his playing hands. She carefully, softly, moved them away from the silver harpstrings. Then she sung, as the waterfall and river, as the wind and the trees, and again, the young man opened his eyes.

She looked upon him. She smiled, knowing that if she slept now, even if she was so near, the forest would embrace him forever. She smiled, singing a part of the song she had heard and loved and would eternally love. She smiled, watching the man she saw and loved the moment her eyes had spotted him. Slowly, as he listened to her song, he, too, began to smile. And slowly, as he listened to her song, he began to sing too. Their two songs made one, and it was far beyond the beauty of the first song. The forest fell in to gold and silver light. The vines and roots that had embraced him loosened, releasing him. For the first time since he came here, he had been disturbed, but he had begun again to love.

And at last, the Maiden could sleep by her beloveds side, and he had continues to sing on for her until she awakened. Together, then, the two sung their song of beauty. The song echoed throughout the world as they left the peaceful forest's shelter. They cared not for disturbance, for nothing was there that could touch the song's peace. Together, the two made an eternal song, unmatched by the sun, unmatched by the moon, unmatched by all the stars and every other song of the past.

In love, they were eternal. And in love, the two would be until the very last of days upon the beauty of the world.

Angel

e marched through the dim light of the halls within the research complex, humming a little tune to kill the eeriness of the place.

Guard-duty was not fun, but interesting. Sometimes frightening in a place like this, but still interesting.

He stopped as he heard footsteps approaching. If it was an intruder, he would need to be prepared. He aimed his heavy assault rifle towards the sound, a distant corner that led to a security complex that not even he had access to.

He recognized the white-clad scientist, sighing in relief and lowering his weapon. A light flickered.

The Scientist eyed the soldier, then gave him a polite smile. "Could you assist us?"

The question startled him. He stared in to the eyes of the woman, in disbelief. Only as the flickering light calmed again he found the courage to answer. "Sure."

The scientist nodded, turning away and motioning him to follow, which he did.

"We need to move and guard a rare subject." She explained coldly.

He merely nodded, his blue eyes locked on the scientist, still in confusion.

They passed the security to the new Area, and he found himself in a bright, white-walled area. His sight moved from iron door to iron door as they passed them.

The scientist stopped, taking out another entry card and opened the door with it.

The soldier's entire body went cold when he peeked in to the room. The walls were a plain white, sending the first chills down his spine, but that was not the reason for his paleness. Surrounded by a band of white-robes, hooked on to several machines, was a weakened, helpless woman, her clothes made of material he did not recognize, and she was winged. The feathers of this woman's wings were brighter than the walls and robes of the scientists, as if they were crying 'we are pure, unlike them'.

The soldier choked at the cold stares of the men and women that had caught this angel-like person. And he gasped for air as he caught sight of her silver eyes, which were silently screaming for help.

Everything seemed stuck in time, waiting for him to do something.

He approached the winged figure, gulping, offering a hand of aid. To his surprise, she took it, even if shakily.

The entire band moved through the complex in terrifying silence. Only the sounds of the machines, still attached to the winged woman, shattered the silence now and then.

They arrived in a room, an actual guest-room, yet still within the horrible complex of white. The soldier was still relieved though. This room was by far more comforting.

He helped the winged woman to the simple bed, then stepped back. The scientists surrounded their subject yet again, but this time to release her from the chains of wire and plugs.

She, even though there was no visible change to expression or body language, was clearly relieved. And her eyes no longer begged for aid.

He wanted to smile, but the cold glances of the white-robes made him shiver. He stepped back, his eyes watching the angel-like woman.

The scientist who had brought him in to this situation stepped up to him, speaking quietly. "Guard her. You will receive all you need by morning."

17

At least she had said 'her' and not 'it'. He nodded, stepping outside, and continued his guard-duty, only in a different way...

It had been the very next day that he had been officially moved to the position in front of that door. The scientists moved in and out, but never with him. He was merely to guard the door if 'she' was to break out. Or if anyone except the specified few were to go in. He and two others were the only ones with access to the door. One of the two was a scientist, the very same woman that had assigned him to this job, and the other another guard who was also pulled off from his post to stand front of the very same plain gate-door the other twelve hours when he himself was off-duty...

On this day, his second day at his new post, he had seen her many times. She was just beautiful, and he told himself that every time he caught a glimpse of her. Two more days passed, no different from the first two, until the fifth day came.

He took a deep breath, then looked at the door behind him. His glance moved away from it, nearly instantly, and began to observe the white halls. His senses tried to detect something. Not an intruder, no, but a scientist.

Nothing. He slung his rifle to his back, pulled out the security card, and opened the iron gate to the angel-woman.

What he saw set him in confusion and awe alike.

The woman was on her knees, her hair nearly touching the cold floor he was sharing. Her head was bowed and her hands were clasped, and his own eyes widened as he heard the voice of this 'angel' sing.

All feelings he had before faded. He fell to his knees, his heart softened to the point that he wished to weep, and yet none of the sung words he could understand.

Joy filled him, even a tear escaped him, and as it flowed down his cheek, finally reaching the white floor, she stopped. Her head rose.

He, still in shock of the feelings, gasped, attempting again and again to say something, yet never managed.

At last she rose, stepped closer to the overwhelmed soldier, then sank again to a crouch. A touch of her fingers on his lips set the entire room into silence. He truly stared at her, her and her eyes of silver, his mind going blank.

All he could realize was the touch and his breathing. Slowly, very slowly, she pulled her hand back. And as slowly, she rose again to her feet. All the while, he still watched those eyes.

Until he heard the distant footsteps of this angel-woman's captors.

Immediately he leapt to his feet, and locked the door. He could see the sorrow of the woman, and regretted never entering the room.

Quickly, he tried to look as if he never had moved, but luck was not on his side. The woman-scientist stepped in front of him, looked up at him and made him feel small. She would have loved to kill him.

"Why have you opened the door to the subject?" she said, while the two other scientists looked as bored as the two guards that were with them.

He had no answer.

"Speak with me!" she shouted. But still he had no answer, and merely fell to a knee, pounding a first to his heart. He did wrong. He knew he did. Of course there had been cameras installed. Of course. He forgot the most obvious. He had been oblivious to the beauty of the woman inside, locked up, saddened…

Spitting some very un-ladylike words, the scientist opened the door, and they all stepped in. The gate closed behind them, leaving the guardsman in shame of his actions.

After what seemed an eternity, though, the band had come back out. He didn't dare look up yet. He noticed how only four set of feet left. The fifth was still around. He noticed the scientist's voice.

"Stand."

He did as commanded, didn't dare look in her eyes.

"Look at me."

Forced by command, he did what he didn't dare on his own.

"You have permission to enter the room once every day for fifteen minutes, no longer, until told."

He blinked. He was allowed to be with the angel? He tilted his head slightly, not noticing, and his professional stance seemed to have faded, for the scientist looked disgusted with her cold, usually emotionless features.

"It seems she trusts you and not us. Now back to your post. And do not dare to let her flee!" she snapped, and then she added cooly: "You would be executed for treason."

Seeing that his life was on stake, he nodded slowly, but did not speak. He knew she was not finished.

"You have not entered the room yet. But remember, this is not for you."

And then she left, spinning at her heels, rushing back to wherever she came from. He wondered, watching after her, subconsciously fiddling with some levers on his rifle, what had happened inside.

A few days had passed, but he just did not seem to dare enter the place, dark compared to the near-white halls where he stood guard. He had thought about her, again and again. He saw her beautiful face, those silver eyes, the long, perfect hair… And the more he thought about it, the more he wondered, and was worried if she looked still same. The scientists came and went, but he did not even care turn and look at her anymore…

Eighteen days had passed since he'd seen her. And he decided to go inside. So he did, opening the heavy, white door, and stepping inside.

He nearly choked, seeing the angel-woman. She looked as beautiful as ever, but even more so tired, exhausted, and she knelt on the cold floor, hands weakly clasped together, head bowed as if it were heavy…

Things were laying in the room, pencils, pens, color… He would have laughed, but it was more frightening, saddening, than funny. He did notice though, that she had used what was given to her. And with closer looking, he saw her fingers had been in the bottles of paint. They were only roughly cleaned, but no less fragile-seeming than before.

He looked around the papers about. He saw things he could read, single letters, though never a word, as if she tried to say something, but not knowing how to word, or spell… or she knew, for he saw things rubbed and lined out until it was unreadable again. But he also saw other things, which looked like mere scribble, done in paint, in complex measure, with, most probably, her bare hands.

But also the walls, as he realized after looking up from the floor, was full of the paint-writing. He was rather shocked, choking again.

She looked up, as if only now noticing him. At first she looked frightened, and began moving away, until he looked at her, set down his rifle, knelt and attempted to look as harmless as he could. He smiled softly, in awe of her beauty, then blushed a little as her fear turned to something more curious.

She was, for all he could tell, a lost child.

21

He held out his hand to her. "I... I won't hurt you." he said softly, honestly. Only hesitantly did she move closer to him, coming on all fours. Her wings spread, and he would have backed off, but he wanted to remain steady, friendly... not feeling threatened or intimidated by her in any way. So she same closer, then very, very carefully, she took his hand. His heart would have stopped that moment. He felt her hands, soft, smooth. It was funny that she still had paint on them, but it didn't matter. He carefully held her hand, then began to examine the paint on it.

She watched him. He knew she did. He felt it; he was trained to know when he was watched like this. She was curious, he was sure. She wanted to know what he was doing, as he wanted to know what she had been doing...

He looked up, giving a friendly smile. "You see... I didn't hurt you."

She looked him right in to the eye, with her silvery, beautiful, yet tired ones... and she nodded softly, as if surprised that he was right. He let go of her. Her hand dropped somewhat, and landed on the floor with a soft 'thud'. The room was darker, but it was better so. It was not blinding.

She watched him, still silent.

He bit his lip, looking around. He seemed to need to somehow make conversation with her. Leaning a little away, he nabbed a piece of paper and a pen that was lying nearby, putting it in front of him. Then he looked up to her again. He had to force himself not to look away, from her face, those eyes... "Can you write?"

She nodded hesitantly, then hesitating again, she pointed in a smooth motion to the walls. He though shook his head, and grabbed another nearby paper, one that had some remains of letters on them. He pointed to the letters. "Alasch. Can you write alasch?" She looked at him, as if pondering whether he should receive this answer or not. Then she nodded, barely seen. His reaction was a brow rising. So she could write. "You can understand me too. And I'm sure you can talk if you wanted to."

She didn't answer. Instead, she took the paper, and started to do something with her hands that looked like writing. The paint on her fingers was dry, but it didn't seem as if she cared. Whatever she was doing, there was no way for him to figure it out.

He sighed softly. He watched her for long moments in silence, watched her touch the paper with her fingers, as if she knew exactly what she was doing, swift and accurate...

He was then lost in the beauty of this woman, uncaring, unnoticing what she was doing. He didn't even truly realize how she got up to get paint, to actually write on the paper. Neither did he realize it when she moved the paper to him. He only did notice when she touched his cheek, and he felt not the soft skin, but the odd, cold paint.

He nearly jumped, staring at her in confusion. She seemed to not notice, or not care, and looked down at the paper she had scribbled with her odd writing.

The blue, still drying paint upon the snow-white, large paper showed a set of her odd writing and under it alaschen letters. He looked up at her, wide-eyed. She had written to him, in two languages, one he had thought was merely scribble, one in Alasch...

The doors slid open. He heard it, the uncomfortable sliding of rubber on stone, even if it was quiet. He closed his eyes. His heartbeat. He heard how she played with the paper. She could not flee, and she knew. She was afraid, he felt that. But she was by far not dumb. They had not known of the existence of such a creature except in mere myth, and myths were something

23

long lost. But now, he stood before something that resembled legend. A beautiful, winged creature. And proof that she was truly what she seemed was her knowledge. He stood, dragging his rifle after himself. Time was up, and they ensured he was following the rules. They asked questions, but he found himself speechless as she was, though, he was sure, for far other reasons…

He had read: 'This is the Angelic Writing.'

The following day he couldn't focus on his duty, not one bit. All he could think about was what he had experienced, in that room with the angel. He hadn't even gotten much sleep because of his thoughts, spinning and spinning that he sometimes felt dizzy, ill. Now, here, in front of her door, it wasn't easier. He touched his cheek that had been painted on the previous day, his stare blank and his thoughts travelling to a very different place and time.

Then he closed his eyes and, for the first time in eight tiring hours, looked at the door. He wasn't quite sure what to do. He was afraid of entering, afraid of seeing that sad face again, of the most beautiful creature he'd ever seen in a state of sorrow and weakness. He was afraid of what she was doing to him, and he was afraid of what was being done to her. He looked at the door, helpless...

A good soldier he had been, fearless. He was sent against a large force of the rebels, and once even to Talae to watch the southern coast. He was known to be brave, without fear even. But then he was here, within white halls where things – no, 'people' – were being researched, and all he knew was worry and fear. He wanted to do something, he wanted to save the angel, wanted to hide her... and he wanted to be alone with her. He wanted things that he shouldn't have. This was for the cause of the Alaschen Empire... Wasn't it? He shivered, watching the door.

An hour later, he opened it, the door, and stepped inside, cautiously, rifle to his back. He saw her, the angel, sitting in the middle of the room, her legs pulled her body, her arms wrapped around them, and her head on her knees, making her hair flow around the floor around her. Her wings, too, were closed and tight on her body. The rifle slowly slid off his shoulder, then fell to the ground. He had it secured, but it made a loud noise still, and the angel tensed, afraid. He looked at his gun, rather in disbelief that he had dropped it, but his thoughts shifted all too quickly back to the angel.

"I-I'm sorry." he said. "I didn't mean to scare you." He watched her. She didn't look up, she didn't turn, she only relaxed slightly, but still was afraid. Dismissing his weapon completely, he approached her in slow steps, until he stood beside her. Hesitant, he moved his hand to set it on the Angel's shoulder. At the touch, she tensed again. "It's all right... I won't hurt you. I promise I won't." He bit his lip after saying that, not able to do much more but watch her. After a while, she opened her eyes, lifted her head, and looked at him with those eyes of purest silver. He couldn't say a word anymore, too lost with the sorrow she spoke with a single look. All he could do, all he could think of doing, was embracing her, giving her some sort of comfort. His hands brushed a set of feathers, making him shiver. But his shivers coming from the unknown were nothing to her silent sobs. He held her more firmly, trying to give her something of his remaining strength, but it helped little. Still, he was too much a stranger to her. Still, she was too much of a mystery, a myth, to him. So, after a while, he let go of her, giving her a little space, and he looked in to her face.

25

His heart almost broke as he saw her tears. "Please... Oh by Eion's Grace, please don't cry..." She looked at him, deep in to his eyes, reaching out to touch him. She held his cheeks, and with all strength that remained within her, she smiled a weak smile. And that, so it seemed, mended his broken heart for a moment. He had almost forgotten what smiling was, and after so much sorrow, seeing her like this was the best thing he could think of happening. "Thank you." he whispered. "Thank you. I'm so sorry. Thank you..." He stood, slowly, and walked away from her, picking up his rifle. He turned back to her for a moment. "I'll be back tomorrow..." And then he left her alone again, frustrated that he had so little time to share...

As promised, he was there the following day. Halfway through his shift, he opened the door to visit her, finding her painting again. He approached her, cautiously, then crouched near her. "You're writing again..." he figured, watching her writing, and her hands, the strange way how she wrote. He couldn't look in her face. That beautiful face. He was too afraid to find sorrow in it again.

He glanced over the many papers instead. Besides the many symbols, letters he didn't know, he could read others, and a set of papers gathered to spell a word: Eion, meaning God. He wondered. He knew she could write his language. Was she really related to Him, Eion, their God? Myth. She would 'have' to be related. "You're... You really 'are' an angel, aren't you?" He now looked at her, at her expression. She was calm, neither in sorrow nor in joy, and was concentrated in writing. She either didn't listen to him, or didn't bother to react to his question. So he watched her, watched her write in that strange language he had no knowledge of.

After a while, she seemed finished writing, and looked to him. Her eyes looked deep in to his soul. He choked at the gaze, and had to turn away. She, though, touched his cheek, and gently turned him to face her again. She then set her new symbols to the other writing that made 'Eion', and looked to him. He was confused, obviously, moving closer to her and the letters on the floor. He opened his mouth to ask, but she quickly set a finger to his lips. He was, truly, lost, and didn't know what he was meant to do. She then set a hand over his eyes, and he closed them. She stood, he felt the soft wind, a streak of hair brushing his face, just barely. He frowned, but a soft touch to his forehead made him relax. His heart beat, quickly, afraid of what she'd do. He was sure, she'd not harm him. It was impossible for him to imagine such thing, but still he had no idea what would await him.

Nothing happened for a while, until he felt the cold touch of ink upon his face. She was… drawing, on him? He twitched a little, not used to the cold, wet paint to his skin, but he tried his best not to move. Then she took one of his hands, very gently, soft, giving him the feeling that she was smooth air rather than an actual person. He tensed, though, as he felt that cold wetness upon his skin again, felt as she drew something upon his hand, then his other hand. Then there was nothing, and she let him go. She touched his eyes again, and he understood, and he opened his eyes.

She looked him over, as if examining what she had done, to be sure that it was all the way it should be, then she gave him a soft smile. He couldn't help but smile back, even if he didn't understand what had just happened. Either way, he felt good, excellent even, not only because of her smile.

She whispered something, quietly, too quiet for him to understand, but it filled his heart with something he hadn't known before, something good, something, that seemed to give him strength. Then she looked to him with a sudden sad face, and looked to the door.

He followed her glance and realized that she was right. It was time again for him to leave. He sighed, but he wasn't sad. He left, and somehow, he had no worries...

Three days passed, he had seen her every one of the days, and she seemed less and less sorrowful each time he came. He still felt the strength from that day she had painted him, and he wondered what that was, because he had found no more trace of the ink on his skin. Despite her being less frightful of him, she still was cautious, and she hadn't come too close to him since those three days past. He decided to try something...

"What's your name?"

Her eyes examined his in both curiosity and fear. She hesitated in answering his question, he could tell.

"I'm here to protect you," he added after a long pause, hoping it would help.

She shifted slightly in her sitting position, tilting her head a little. Her golden hair dropped off her shoulder, creating an unnoticed wind.

He watched her, smiling, small but happily. But in the same instant his expression changed to something sad.

The angel-woman took a deep breath.

"You are sad?" Her voice was truly an angel's, but it shook and was unsteady.

He smiled again. Finally, finally she spoke. "Not anymore," was his honest reply, honesty a habit that was drilled in to him. "Well…" He had to think of what to say, his expression turning thoughtful. Finally he said: "It's sad to see you locked up here, I mean, it's creepy and they treat you like some lab rat." Though he hadn't seen any scientists during his shift in a while.

She bowed her head in sorrow, as if in agreement.

With a sigh, he stood, and slowly marched towards the door that he was meant to guard. Every hour, minute, even second that he stood at that door, he liked the research base less and less. In fact, he began to hate those scientists. He knew that they would love to take the angel-woman apart. That image was paining.

Before he opened the door, he glanced back at the woman, examining her. He would also like to know what she was and how she worked, but most of all he wanted to know *who* she was.

Her glance met his. He immediately turned, and opened the door. The hall's light was immensely brighter than the inside, killing his eyesight for a moment. "I'll be there for you," he promised. "Whenever I can, I will be there to help you." He closed his eyes for a moment, then looked back to her. "For you. But no matter how much I hate it, I will need your help, too."

She looked at him, her pure, silver eyes telling him how confused and lost she was. He pondered for a moment, before explaining. "Can you tell me what they do to you? Maybe I can explain it, and make it less frightening. I don't visit you because I have to, but because I want to. And I leave not because I want to, but because I have to if I want to see you again. All I wish... is to help you."

She looked at him for long moments, reading his expression. Then, in the end, she smiled, and she said in her beautiful voice: "I will wait for you every passing day and every passing night, and I will tell you of the burdens upon my body, my heart and my mind, and I will let you aid me. It will soothe both our souls, I am sure."

He shivered upon the voice. The first words she had spoken were already beautiful, but the following made him only realize that there were no words to describe what he had heard.

He bowed to her, placing his hand to his heart, in all honors devoting himself to her, no matter what the cost. He stayed bowed, maybe a minute, maybe ten, before rising and stepping out of the room, closing the door and taking his rifle back in hand.

Day after day he then visited her, always during the same time. She told him what they did to her. In the beginning he had problems to understand, because she had no clue what names the tools had. He explained it to her, day after day, until she could tell him in whole what was happening to her. In general, so it seemed, the scientists only asked questions, took samples of her skin, her hair, her feathers, her blood, checked her internal functioning under the conditions she was in. It seemed that, while not cutting her open and seeing what was inside, thus possibly killing her, they still wished to know how she worked not only physically, but also mentally. It relieved the guardsman, and it made the angel less afraid knowing what was happening to her.

"This day," she began, "they brought me to a place, it was dark. They had brought me there before, when they first had caught me. Because I knew what they wanted, I did it. They let these machines rotate around me, and made pictures of inside of me. Then they put plugs on my head and asked questions. I felt dizzy, I think I passed out too." The soldier was a little worried, sitting in arm's reach of her on the cold ground. "The last part was, I think, testing your brainwaves to know how your body, your brain, rather, reacts to different stimuli." He frowned, but she touched his forehead and made it go away. She did it often, but he couldn't help but smile every time she did.

"Don't frown," she said. She said it often, too, and his answer was always the same. "I try." He watched her, her beauty that couldn't be described, that strength in her that grew with every day passing. Only after a struggle he could get his eyes off her, looking at his arm watch. He still had time...

She tilted her head, wondering what was coming now. He pondered, and decided to ask something he hadn't asked in far too long. "What's your name?" She didn't answer, just smiled. It was quiet for a long moment. All she did was brush her long hair back, shift her wings a little. It seemed she was pondering, all the while watching him. And he watched her, not sure what to feel or think while he was waiting, no, *hoping* for an answer. "Vilnae," she then said all of a sudden. He frowned again, not sure if that was a word or a name, until she touched his forehead again, speaking on. "That is the name I was given." Curiosity struck the soldier, and, removing his frown, he instantly asked: "By whom?" She removed her hand, smiling at him again. "Lord Eion Lysnith."

He blinked at her. Right. He remembered the myths, somewhat, of the Angels and Eion. He still couldn' t believe the myths were quite true, though, so he frowned again. This time she wouldn't touch his forehead. Instead, he made a sad face. It made him lose his frown too, but he didn't smile. Instead he took her hands, frail things that he sometimes was afraid to hold, and asked her what was wrong.

"You don't believe me, either." she said simply, her silver gaze distant upon the ground beside him, her hair softly touching his skin, making him shiver. "I-I'm sorry," he said in honesty. "They were stories told to me, and they were stories meant to be nothing more but that – stories. I'm sorry. Forgive me." He bowed his head, letting go of her hands. But she took his an instant after, looking at him again. He looked up to her, a worried look upon his face, but he couldn't help but curse himself for his petty worries after seeing her expression, sorrowful. Despite all the strength he helped her gain, she was still as frail as she looked. But she smiled, a soft, cautious smile, and strengthened the grip on his hands, like giving him the strength that she lacked in that moment. He looked at her, in wonder, then after a bit, with a smile. "Thank you," he said. "And I thank you," she answered. He gave her a questioning look, she, though, shook her head. "You see me as I am, and you strengthen me to endure this all. That is worth all thanks I could ever give."

He looked away from her, touched by this, truly, deep within his soul. Repeating what she had said in his mind several times, he closed his eyes, smiled, then faced her again, opening his eyes again to look right into hers. "I took a vow, and I took it because I mean it." He paused, trying to think of what to say, observing those eyes of silver that saw through him, that saw right into his heart, his soul. Even if it frightened him being so incredibly open to her, he couldn't look away.

"You have no idea what you give me in return," he admitted, then, and finally closed his eyes. He was hit by surprise, then, when she embraced him, carefully, softly. He felt her skin against his cheek, some of her weight upon his shoulders, strands of hair that had found their way to his open hands. He felt the shifting of her weight as she breathed and as her wings moved. And in this very moment, he couldn't have been more aware that the myth was all too real, because he felt her soft touch, smelled her sweet scent, heard her quiet breath. And in that moment, he couldn't say how incredibly true his admittance was. She gave him more than anyone could ever imagine.

"I don't want you to go away." That sentence startled him. He opened his eyes, looking at the wall that way behind her, painted in many symbols, probably even entire sentences.

"I'm..." He wanted to say that he was sorry, that he had no choice, and all he could do was make a sad face, because he really could stay, just, he would need to live with the consequences. And the consequences would be rather fatal...
"I... have a choice, but in the end..." His voice was shaking. "I-I wish there was a way. A way for me to stay without consequences in the end." He leaned his head against hers. His entire body seemed to lose strength. She tightened the embrace, her wings spreading a little. "What would they do to you?" she asked quietly. He was silent for a very long time, wondering what he should say, and how. In the end, he stayed with the absolute truth. "They'd execute me." "Just for staying with me?" He couldn't help but frown again. It was a good question, a very good question, really, one that he hadn't asked himself yet. So, again he answered with full honesty. "I-I don't know, really. I think so, though."
Her grip on him tightened more, and more, too did her brilliant white wings spread. Slowly, cautiously, he lifted his arms to return the embrace, his touch first careful, as if he were afraid to break her, then stronger, and stronger, until he clung on to her as she did on to him. "I don't like this place!" she shouted, surprising him completely, because he had never thought that she was able to shout. "I don't like this place." she repeated, almost in a whisper. He felt helpless. There was nothing he knew he could do to help her out of this misery. A thousand thoughts, ideas, rushed through his mind, but more than half of them ended in his sure death, and the other half would too, in time, be his end, if not hers, too.
"I'm so sorry." It was all he knew he could say. He suddenly felt her entire weight upon him. He threatened to fall over, backwards, but held against the weight. "I'm... so sorry." he repeated. "I need to go, though..." "I don't want you to leave!" Her voice sounded desperate. It made him feel worse, far worse

33

than he felt already. He had to laugh, a sad laugh, suddenly aware of how fast his feelings could change, from joy to paining sorrow.

He felt miserable, stupid, even. For a moment, he regretted his vows, regretted ever existing, but then it was the Angel's – no, what was her name? Vilnae? - Vilnae's sorrows that made him shove all that he felt, hated, feared in to some distant corner of his inner self. "I promised to be there for you. Even if we don't see each other. I will still be there."

He slowly let go of her, and he felt that she, too, released her grip on him. He set his hands on her shoulders, seeing her head bowed. "Please look at me," he asked, and she raised her head, showing him her face, her eyes that were wet and showed some sort of longing. "Please, please don't be sad." She swallowed down her worries, took a deep breath to gain new strength, then nodded, and in proof, she gave him a soft smile. He could never grow tired of those, could not stop wishing that this smile would never go away. He nodded, returning the smile with a soft one of his own. He looked at her, examined her face, then tore himself away from her and stood.

"You told me your name. It was Vilnae, right?" She nodded. He took a breath, proud of remembering it. "My name's Jachil, Jachil Delnay." He gave her another smile, a true one, then stepped over to the door, opening it, pausing for a moment, then leaving the room. "Vilnae." He said there, out in the white halls that were brighter than day. Holding his rifle ready, he heard the door close on its own. His smile was gone, and he feared the next hours that were to come, knowing they would be dreadful torture.

He had... fallen in love.

His entire life had suddenly become hell, except for those few moments he could share with the angel Vilnae. It had already been months since he had first seen her, and he would never have thought how she would affect him, a once so disciplined soldier. Not a single moment passed where he didn't think of her. Not a minute without his heart aching. He suffered for three days until he decided to seek the scientist that was working on Vilnae, the woman that had given him the job to guard that damned door. He had to have a serious talk with that woman that he learned to hate without seeing her. He had to talk to her before he went insane.

Changing shifts with another soldier he never talked to, not even looked at more than he needed to, he went to search for that accursed woman's office, stepping through the white halls, passing by a single light that flickered for a moment, turned left... Then he stood there, in front of a door that couldn't have been more simple. It felt out of place, here, where there were dozens and dozens of doors that couldn't even be opened with powerful explosives. He stared at it with an expression of disgust, stepped a single step closer to it, raised his hand and knocked.

"Come in," he heard from inside. He turned the knob and stepped inside the white room. All that made it different form the outside was that it was dimmed, that it had a desk and a computer and a few sets of drawers on one wall. Otherwise the room was as eerie and dead as the outside. "Captain Jachil Delnay requesting to speak openly, miss," he said, but he didn't salute, didn't stand firm. It didn't matter. The woman had her back turned to him and seemed busy with other things. "Permission given, soldier." He was slightly surprised. He had expected to disrespect his authorities and speak without being allowed to. But this made things easier.

35

"I want Vilnae – the angel – I want her set free." He tensed now, waiting for a reaction, but he didn't get any until the woman was done doing whatever she was doing and turned around to face him, pushing her glasses back in to position. "Why should we do such thing, Captain?" she asked simply, watching him with her cold eyes, but there was no anger, no surprise, nothing.

"Because she is breaking here in imprisonment." The woman seemed to actually consider his words, then shook her head. "Testing the subject under extreme stress will aid our research. There is no reason to let her go." He tensed. "Th-then I wish to see her more often. Longer."

Now the woman raised a brow. "What gain would we have from this?" He snorted. "She doesn't go mad, or tries to break free when she has the chance? She doesn't try to kill herself, or hurt someone else?" He didn't know, and those were just wild ideas that came to his mind. The scientist pondered this, too, but she still had other questions. "And what would *you* gain from it?" Nothing, he tried to answer. Honor, he tried too. But it wouldn't come out of his mouth either. Service to the Lord was another option, but it wasn't his intention. So he had to stick with truth, even if he was afraid to speak it openly. "My own sanity."

For the first time since he had met this woman, he saw some human expression that wasn't filled with anger or general fury. She smirked. "So the Captain admits his feelings. I was afraid you'd go on suicide before you would." What? He had expected many answers, but that was not one of them, absolutely not. There was no way he could hide his surprise. The woman clarified the situation for him. "We've observed you, Captain, ever since I've allowed you to see the subject." Observed. Of course they were watching his every damned step for months, and he didn't even damned notice. He cursed himself, cursed these people, cursed everything until he had no more words to use. He was just another subject. Observations of what happen to those that get too close to her, he supposed. He was angry, so incredibly angry, he just wanted to shout, he wanted to hurt these people, he wanted-

But no. All he did was make a fist, so tight that his entire arm was shaking. He stayed quiet despite all the rage that was within him. He was, somewhat, in control of himself. "Do I... get permission or not?" he then asked, trying to not sound too harsh. The scientist observed him, again giving him that considering look. "Considering that you are a valuable member of the Military Union, of the Empire, really, I think I will allow you to see her more. Ah, I know. You can see her after your shift."

After his shift? His fist slowly released itself. He wondered. Did she mean the entire time he was off-duty? She didn't say for how long, so he could assume it. This... rather shocked him. "Go on, see her, then, Captain." She motioned him to leave, waving him away with her hand. He stepped back a few steps, spun around, and he hurried. Being turned in to a subject or not, being angry for as much as he could care, it all mattered nothing knowing that he had gotten something he desired dearly. The only thing he hadn't considered was the other guardsman that didn't let pass. "I've permission to enter!" Captain Delnay said, but the other guardsman didn't let him in. "I've yet to hear that officially," was the only reply he got. The Captain stepped back.

Fine... Fine. It hurt him incredibly, now, so close to seeing her again, but he turned away, and made his way home in deep sorrow.

His shift at end, he opened the door and closed it right behind him. His rifle he had left outside, he didn't need it in here. He spun around and looked at her, the angel, Vilnae, his heart finally at ease. She looked up at him, first frightened, then, slowly, with time, more relaxed. She stood, her entire set of robes flowing with the movement, and she approached him, every step in perfection, placing him already in awe. She stopped, so close to him that his heart threatened to stop, so close that he ceased to breathe, so close that she needed only to lean a little closer to hold him tightly. He closed his eyes as she did, and his heart beat again and his breath came again. He placed his arms around her, carefully. "I'm sorry I'm late." he said quietly to her. She let go of him, just a little, to be able to look in to his eyes.

"Why did it take you so long?" she asked after having her glance returned. He pondered for a moment, looking for the best way to explain. "I had to make sure that we can see each other for longer." Her eyes suddenly seemed to have an inner sparkle. "You do not have to leave?" He shook his head. "Almost. I can stay here half of the day. The other half I have to guard you from outside." She held him tight, so tight he thought she'd never let go of him again. "Thank you," she said quietly, and her voice was filled with joy. He just smiled. Here, he was at peace, no matter if he was observed or not.

It took her a while, but eventually, she let him go. She pulled him to the middle of the room, then pulled him down, sitting, so he sat, too. And now, that she knew they had much time together, he could see her entire curiosity, almost childish. She was like a brilliant star, a radiant sun, and he didn't dare speak a word, so much he respected her presence, and her beauty was beyond what he could have imagined. Those brilliant white feathers of hers, they shone with a light of their own, and that smile gave him so much joy that he felt unworthy of it. He couldn't help, as she took his hands, but to cry in joy. He couldn't stop the tears, even though he couldn't comprehend why they came. And she wiped the tears away, and he knew that there were no words worthy of her.

"Jachil, please, please tell me of your people," she asked a while later. He wasn't all too sure of what she meant, was even ashamed of not getting it, and he had to ask. "What do you mean by my people?" "The Alasch," she answered. "I only saw very little of it, but the little I saw was very different from this place. So tell me, please, Jachil, tell me of your people." He found this rather interesting, but equally, he wanted to give her whatever she wanted. "I'm not sure where to begin," he admitted, and thinking about it, it really wasn't that easy to explain the entire Empire. He frowned, receiving a chuckle, and a touch. "You frown too much," she realized, and he smiled.

He did his best to explain as much as he could during the next few hours, talking of the technology they had gathered, telling her of the Lord, their Emperor, and of the Mages and the mystic warriors that were the Alaschen Elite. And he told her of cars, and airplanes, of satellites and broadcasts, of schools, universities. He told her of the daily life of a civilian, and of the daily life of a soldier. And in the end, he also told her of the holy priesthood.

Vilnae made a bit of a sad face when he was finished. Before he could ask, she gave him an answer already. "Eion Lysnith sent me to deliver a message to one of his priests," she said. "I got tired and needed to take a rest, because Aerinoth is a big world, and I can only fly so far. And then something stung me, and I fell asleep, and when I was awake, I was in this place."

He listened to her, and somehow he wanted to undo what had happened, but there was no way he could, so he felt somewhat frustrated. Then he actually thought of what she had said. "You were... supposed to deliver a message? What message?" The question came before he could think further on. Vilnae shook her head. "I do not know what was in the message, I only know I should have delivered it a long time ago." She smiled a little. "Eion Lysnith will not be happy, but he will be even less happy for missing me at his court."

His court... He felt, all of a sudden, so small, so worthless. He was afraid, very afraid. What was he worth in her eyes, in her world? He didn't know. He feared the worst. What was he worth? He looked sad, depressed. She didn't like that. She was worried. "Jachil?" She spoke softly, touching his cheeks just barely with the tips of her fingers. He shuddered, looking in to her eyes, those silver eyes that could make all the bad in his heart go away. "Tell me, please, what is wrong?" He fought for words. He didn't know if he should bother her with his petty worries. He didn't know if, at this moment, he even had any worries. "I'm lost," was all he could say, his voice slightly pitched. She closed her eyes, and leaned her forehead against his, caressing his cheeks with her soft hands. "Then I will try to bring you back," she promised.

Later, it felt like days, she let go of him again. He felt refreshed, renewed. He felt unbreakable, untouchable. He had no worries, no doubts, nothing left within himself but the joy of being near her. He couldn't comprehend what she had done to him, but it mattered little, really. It was just important that it had happened at all. She was tired, obviously, and it was getting late. She threatened to fall asleep on him, so he lifted her, for the first time truly bearing her entire weight, and set her on the bed that was in the room. He had never seen her on it. Maybe she had never used it, or she merely preferred the floor over the cushions. He didn't know. He watched her open her eyes for a moment more to look at him before closing them again, putting a smile on her face. And half-covered, half-clinging on to the sheets, her wings finding a place untouched, she seemed to fall asleep in sheer exhaustion.

He smiled. He could have stood there and watched her until the very last of his days. But he had a duty to fulfil. It was his shift now. So, slightly sad, but only slightly, he left the room, eyes closed to not hurt them, and took a breath. When he opened his eyes again he was ready to guard her. He was not separated from her, no, he was doing his duty for her. And he did it with pride.

Every passing day he learned of things completely new to him. She had described him the heavenly City of Vael'alath, told him of the great god Eion Lysnith and his court, explained to him how the Priesthood functioned. She began teaching him her language, teaching him how to speak with the right pitch and length, showed him how to write with the right thickness and depth. In exchange, he told her all he knew of the Empire, drawing her the many things that seemed unthinkable to live without in daily life, and explaining so much of what he had learned He told her what he knew of the places he had seen in the world. He described the wondrous Capital City, the great desert of Selt, the strange ocean of Talae and the little he had seen of the frightening isle named Dark Wing. Curious, as they both were, they learned more of each other, their cultures and also the work they had. Captain Jachil Delnay was a soldier, he was part of the Military Union and he lived and died for the Lord and the Empire. Vilnae was a messenger, one of Eion Lysnith's swiftest, and she was his most beloved of angels. She, too, would live and die for her master, her god, but it was not her duty.

41

Jachil had been thoughtful, one day. Her blessings upon him, there was no way he could be in sorrow, but he remained to wonder and to worry. "Say, Vilnae, if you're Eion's dearest angel, why doesn't he come here to rescue you?" It was rather disrespecting to disbelieve in a god and his power, but he had to know. The angel looked sad. "We are deep below the ground, aren't we?" He pondered on it for a bit, then nodded. For a base of this kind, it was rather deep, yes. "It's about a hundred lengths below surface, and the complex is spread over three floors. We're in the middle one."

She looked at the ceiling with some sort of longing. "They said they wanted to know how strong my wings are, but there is no space to try it beside the surface. You see, we walk only rarely the mortal world and mortal earth. Most of my time I am in the air, where I feel the wind upon my skin, where I feel it break through my feathers." She fully spread her wings, for the first time since he had known her. He stumbled back, in awe of the size that he hadn't really taken notice of. Her wing-span covered the entire length of the room.

Seeing his surprise, she folded them again. "I'm sorry, I didn't mean to frighten you." He shook his head, took a breath in recover and then smiled. "Don't worry about me. You were telling me something. Please, go on." With a nod, she did.

"Eion Lysnith sees his people and he sees his servants. But he only sees them if they do not hide from him. We, here, now, are so far below the sacred ground that he could not find me, not even notice a trace of my being here." She bowed her head for a moment. "And that is why I was lost and unable to return to Eion Lysnith's court."

He wished a way to help her, but he was still selfish enough to know that this sort of suffering brought the two of them together. "So to get home, you'll need to reach the surface."

She nodded. "For sure, Eion Lysnith would bring me back the moment I could breathe the surface's air again." He took her hands, looked deep in to her eyes with a smile, and he said: "I will bring you there, even if it takes me all eternity. I will bring you there, I promise, back to freedom where you belong." Her eyes were wide and slowly filled with so much joy that he was close to tears. He lived not for the Lord, not for the Empire, but he lived, now, only for her. She put a tight grip on his hands, her smile so grand he couldn't have felt more joyful. And she laughed, and she looked him in the eye and he had to share her joy even more. "I thank you, Jachil Delnay, for that is the greatest gift one could give me here. If not by Eion Lysnith's Will, then by my own, I will wish you no less than freedom, too, and if not by Eion Lysnith's will, then by my own, I will wish you no less than the sweetest of blessings that I may give." And she let go of his hands, holding his face instead, her touch careful, and she pulled him closer and gave him a soft kiss upon his forehead. His eyes closed for a moment.

She smiled upon him, and he opened his eyes, feeling that smile. Nearly overwhelmed with things he could barely name, he was with her, and he wished to eternally have it stay that way. He wondered what she was thinking about, wondered what it was she felt. He could ask, and she'd say simple things as 'I am happy' or 'I am worried', in rare times even 'I am sad', but what her thoughts were remained unknown to him. And even at the times he did ask, the answer did not satisfy him, for she had said that it was too complex for his language.

He took one of her hands, kissing her palm. Wide-eyed, she watched him, watched as his head rose, and watched as his pale eyes searched hers. And she smiled.

"Tell me more of your language," he bid. And because it was his wish, she nodded, and she gathered papers both empty

43

and written on, and then she showed him more of the Angelic Tongue that was spoken by her and her race.

Five days he spent intensely learning the unknown language, five days during which he slept far too little, standing guard or being with the Angel. Five days, and each time he wasn't within her room, he was trying to come up with a plan on how to get her out of here. He wasn't in a hurry, but he still was afraid that he might lose her one day. And every day he didn't try to find a way to save her was a day wasted. But then came the one day when, despite all, he couldn't do a thing. He was talking to her, trying to use her language, and they had a good time because she constantly corrected him. Then, all of a sudden, soldiers entered, and with them two of the scientists. Their appearance was so sudden that it startled the captain. He was up to his feet, reflexes telling him to reach for the weapons he had taken off; they were laying at the other side of the room. These reflexes caused the other soldiers to rush at him, knock him against the wall behind him and hold him back as the angel – Vilnae – was forced along. He shouted, yelled, struggled. He knocked one of the other soldiers down, forcing the second that held him to use rather drastic measures, and in the end, the captain had a gun at his temple.
While Vilnae had been taken away, the female scientist, all too familiar, turned around and simply said: "Arrest him." The soldiers didn't hesitate. He felt a strong blow upon his head and within a moment, everything turned black and cold.

He opened his eyes, slowly. With rising consciousness, he felt a throbbing pain behind his eyes, and decided to close them again, whilst covering his face with his hands. He waited several moments, then tried to open his eyes again. He stared upon a grey ceiling. He sat up, slowly, and figured, he was on an uncomfortable thing that was supposed to be a bed. And straight across him was another wall, just as there was to his right. So he looked left, and saw strong iron bars. He remembered having guarding several prisons before, but he had never done anything that made him go behind these bars. Well, until now. He attempted to remember what had happened. And as he tried, his heart began to ache and he felt heavy, so incredibly heavy.

"Vilnae," he whispered quietly. He spun on the bed to sit more or less comfortably, even though the action was subconscious, then covered his face with his hands again. It had nothing to do with his headache, nor with the half-light that was rather disturbing. It was a pain that sat very deep and that he had no words for. The closest thing was endless worry.

He heard heavy footsteps, steps that were like every other soldiers' who was on patrol. Still, he looked up. He waited to see the soldier who would pass by. He waited, then saw the youngster, staring straight ahead. The soldier was afraid, he could see it, but did his best to still do his job. He probably just finished the Academy. His grades had to be great then, surely, that they sent him here. That, or so horrible that he was damned to guard some prisoners. The young soldier passed by, and he, Jachil Delnay, held his face again in frustration. A short distraction. But only that.

Hours seemed to have passed. It could have been days though. Or minutes. It didn't matter. Restless, he stood, and started to walk around his cell. There was nothing he could do. Nothing. With passing time, he started to try to occupy himself with more than just wandering through the little space he had. He did push-ups, sit-ups. He practiced the language Vilnae had taught him, recited songs and poems. He even sparred with an

45

invisible enemy. But then he ran out of ideas what to do. He tried to sleep, but that was impossible. In the end, he just was there, existed, worried to death.

And finally, when he was completely exhausted, his door was opened. He was tired, so it took him a while to realize. He looked to the door, saw the young and nervous soldier. "You're to leave the base."

Was he now? He got up and stepped outside his cell, waited for the young soldier to lock the prison again, then followed him, to a lift, stepping inside and going up, up, up - but he didn't want to go up. He looked at the nervous sob. He'd need to decide now. So he waited several floors, before he made a choice. He didn't care for the Lord, the Empire. He didn't care for science or anything else. He didn't give a damn about religion or belief. All he cared for was Vilnae. In a swift motion, he pulled the young soldier's gun out of his holster. "Forgive me," he said, before using it to knock the boy out. Then he stopped the lift, used the emergency exit to get into the shaft. He looked in the dim light for the ladder, and found it after he got used to the dark. He took a deep breath. There was no going back now.

He climbed all the way down, down to the second lowest level. He reached for the number-pad that was there to manually open the door in emergencies. And to him, this *was* an emergency. The door slid open, accepting his code. So, he climbed over to the open door and looked through the white halls, so bright and dead that it was sickening. There was no patrol here, yet, to his luck, but all too soon he'd come across a camera. He needed to be very lucky now. He hoped his determination was enough.

He ran through the white halls, passing countless doors. He never wondered what was behind them, not until now. But he had no time. Neither did he have the intention to save every locked-up creature that was in here. He came to the right crossing, peeking around the corner to see the soldier that took the second shift. He didn't want to do this. He didn't. But the man was too far down to disable. He could only hope to kill him with a good shot. Or maybe-

He looked around the corner again. The soldier stood ready, staring straight ahead. Jachil stepped far enough into the hallway to aim, then he shot. The soldier collapsed, gasping. The sound of the shot, though, echoed and echoed through the halls

He ran to the soldier, looking for the access cards. He slung the man's heavy rifle over his shoulder, stole the man's armor and helmet, checked if the man was still alive after this. He lived, to his relief, even if so just barely. So then tore a part off his shirt and at least tried to stop the man from bleeding to death. He had hit the man's neck in an attempt to not kill him. He hoped someone would save him quickly enough...

That done, he used the stolen card to open the door. The door slowly opened, and revealed the darkened room, Vilnae staring at the the ground in sorrow. She looked up to see what was there, and suddenly, her eyes brightened. "Jachil Delnay," she spoke softly. He nodded, holding out his hand. "We have to be quick, follow me, now!" She was confused, but stood, and took his hand. In a rush, he ran. She looked back to see the wounded soldier, in shock, but didn't say anything, just running with him. Around the second corner, Jachil spotted a barricade as he had expected. He hated this, hated fighting against those he once had trusted, who had once trusted him. But for her, for Vilnae, he'd kill the Lord himself if he needed to.

Several shots fired. The vest he wore just barely saved him from being killed. He looked to Vilnae, breathless. "You... You need to reach the elevator. The door is open. You need to climb the ladder to the top. There you should be close enough to the surface to go home." He had a determined expression, the determination of someone that was ready to die, die for a reason. Vilnae didn't like that expression. "But-" He put a hand at her lips. "Just go. It's for your freedom. I have none anymore, the very least I can do is return what was taken from you!"

Silently, her silver eyes stared in to his. Silently, she took his hand from her lips, and silently she placed a careful kiss upon his. Silently, she nodded. And silently, his determined expression flew away, showing, even if just for a moment, one of bliss. He spun around the corner and begun firing at the half-dozen men that were between him and what he knew as freedom. He moved closer, keeping a constant fire on them. All his hopes were now that Vilnae did what she should while he distracted the soldiers. Then his rifle only clicked. The soldiers came out of their cover, and there was heavy fire upon him. His vest would only hold so much. He used his remaining pistol to fire back, but soon enough, there was only pain in his body. Pain, blood, the rush of battle. A few lengths before the barricade, he began to lose consciousness, and a step later, he only knew pain and darkness.

A soft touch was upon his cheeks, and a soft kiss upon his lips.

He opened his eyes, looking upon a beautiful face, with the most beautiful eyes and most perfect of features. He smiled up at the face, the face he knew that he loved. He felt as if he was floating, he felt as if there were no burdens, nor anything else. All he could do was smile.

"Lord Eion Lysnith thanks you for saving me, Jachil

Delnay. He thanks you with the greatest of gifts he can give to his people." He had heard her speak, but it took him a while to understand what she had said. And even after he had understood it, he wasn't quite sure what it meant, nor did he remember what had happened. He only remembered her, her face, her hair, her arms, her body. He remembered her sweet voice, her joy. And then he remembered her sorrows. And with that memory, his eyes widened more and more as he remembered what had happened.

He was just about to say something, but was silenced with another kiss. She shook her head, letting go of his face. He closed his eyes. He heard her leave, and wondered, wondered what gift he'd get. He stopped feeling as if he was floating, instead feeling the soft breeze of the wind upon his skin. Then he felt the grass, and he felt the cold. He opened his eyes, and he looked up to the bright sky. A cloud was passing by, covering the sun that tried to break through it. He wondered, and wondered more. He sat up. He looked around. He spotted a motorbike that looked somewhat like his. So he stood. He sat on it, and looked around. He had the feeling he knew this place, a large national park not too far away from the Capital City, so he started driving into the direction that he thought was right. And on the horizon he saw the grand metropolis.

He wondered. Was it all a dream? If so, it was a long dream, one of the most frightening dreams he had ever had, but also one of the most beautiful dreams he had ever had. He wondered until he was within the deep heart of the metropolis, in front of a large complex of appartments. He found his keys in his pocket, so he entered, and went up to the eighteenth floor, unlocking the door to his room. Everything was as he remembered... plain, simple. But something was out of place. He approached the thing that lay upon the table in his kitchen, and lifted it. And as he lifted it, he smiled. It was a large feather, so white that it shouted 'I am pure!', and he closed his eyes. His life was now very complicated. But it was worth it. For her. For Vilnae.

Last and Eternal

The young tribeswoman walked along an ancient path, at the foot of her home, the great mountains near the greater White City of Merless. She walked along the path, the long, cold path, and memories of her childhood came in to her mind, of how she and her parents walked the same path, and of how they had told her stories of the eternal Flame-Bird, the Phoenix that protected them – the bird that gave her tribe its name.

She remembered the first day of when she was left alone. She was the last, the last of the proud Phoenix Tribe. And she ensured that her tribe would not be forgotten easily. And Vinnel, she just returned from one of those tasks, returned from Merless and the storytelling within it, returned to rest from the performance, she returned home.

Slowly she stepped on. She smiled, was happy. She was alone, but she couldn't be happier at the same time. She knew, she was not as alone as she always thought. There always was the Firebird's ever-living cousin nearby, watching over her, protecting her. It did not wish for the Phoenix Tribe to end. It fought for her, with her. It gave her the feeling of comfort, of company. And that was why she was smiling.

As she stepped on, she danced, and sung a melody, strong, proud, something that those in Merless would not forget. She ensured they remembered that there once had been the Phoenix Tribe, and that it will not die so easily, as the bird itself never truly fades. She sung her songs of their past glory, of the near and the far. She loved song, music, dance, so duty was passion, was love.

She wandered upon the ancient road up to the mountain, wandered to higher places, to colder places, even though winter was yet to come. She wandered through those higher regions, and up to a cliff, to look down upon the far world. The Sky, clearer than ever, the Sun, setting behind the horizon, letting the Heavens burn in its light, the rocks, trees, cities below, it was a sight to make her smile even more, and make another song, a song of the worlds, of freedom, of the people, of nature, a song that none would remember or hear.

But one, she did know, one would remember. And if it lie within its power, so would she, for all time, remember. The Phoenix was watching, singing with her. Maybe silent, maybe with a voice that no mortal could hear, but it sang, and she felt it in her heart. So even in complete loneliness, she never felt alone. Her guardian shared her love, and would so, for the Last of its children, for all Time, for Eternity.

Daemonblood

 ryr, the white-haired stranger, seated himself in the darkest corner of the tavern which he could find. He felt better if none saw his face, his eyes, his hair, or his hands, all hidden behind his grey clothes. He was more comfortable when none would talk to him, none would notice him, when none would step too close to him.

But he was in a tavern, and everything that was still and silent and wished to be unnoticed made people curious. But in this tavern, relaxed and noble, as it seemed, no curious young girl or backstabbing thugs came, nor did any of the tavern's guards, which he would have expected. No. Instead, in this tavern, he was approached by a noble elf, in beautiful, white clothes, which at the same time seemed so simple.

She was no enemy, also not someone that would become a fiend. She was not beautiful, but far too close to it, and she was calm and relaxed, and smiled as she stopped at his table.

"May I sit with you?" she asked politely. Usually the women just sat and blabbed his ears full, asked all sorts of questions until he left, disgusted. He was glad that it was not the case this time.

With a silent nod and a motion with his hand towards the nearby chair, she sat down.

Again she spoke, again politely, but not with false politeness. If it was played, then she was the best actor he had ever seen in his oh so many years. "May I offer you a drink?"

He pondered a short moment, then nodded. And with equal politeness, yet with some sense of respect, he answered: "Please. And I will pay for you and me."

She shook her head, but ordered, as if reading his thoughts, a fine wine for him. For herself, she ordered some water. He wondered why she would not take any wine, but this stranger, as he, so it seemed, did not wish to be disturbed too much. So he held back the question he wanted to ask. He asked rarely enough anyway. It did not matter.

As their drinks arrived, the young (or so it seemed) elf turned again to him. "What is your name?"

He hesitated. His name was known amongst her race, as also the race of his father, and thus it was dangerous. But somehow this elf managed to awaken his trust. It was rare, but even more rare was this trust confirmed. Not everyone learned out of errors. And he knew, he himself would never learn. "Aryr." Her smile did not fade. It just turned more beautiful. "Then you are the Legendary, are you not? He, whose blood most of our kind does not like." she spoke in a soft voice.

She knew him, and he was confused. Why was she then so friendly? Most would have drawn their weapons by now and would have attempted to murder him on the spot. But not she. Why? He had to ask. "You are not full of hatred towards my name. Why is that so?" He tried to sound friendly. Somehow, he managed.

Still, her smile remained. "Why should I judge someone by his parents?" she spoke in great wisdom. And so he believed that the trust he gave her was no mistake.

He nodded slightly, playing with his full glass of wine. He did not feel the smooth glass through his grey leather gloves. He wondered, though, how it felt.

After a long silence she spoke on. "Why have you chosen this place? Is it not more of a danger if you remain here?"

Somehow she was right. Somehow. But somehow also not. It was more dangerous out there. A lot more.

"No." he said strongly. "It is more safe with many, even when those themselves might be a great threat to me."

She nodded, apparently understanding, then took a sip out of her cup. And then she was silent. It was unnatural, yet not discomforting. Her smile never faded, also not the calm presence around her. She was relaxed and friendly. She did not mock him, did not despise him, did not hate him. In the silence within the entire tavern, he wondered who she was.

"You have never said your own name, dear elf." She laughed quietly. "Forgive me!" she said in a tone which truly was proof that she was sorry. "I call myself Silverstar, as many others call me, for that is my name."

The way she introduced herself reminded him of a faraway time, a distant culture, a distant race which he thought was long dead.

Silverstar, then. A name self-given or chosen, and then accepted. Every name he had chosen for himself felt like a lie. He was never part of that culture, that race.

How would he?

He nodded slightly. Her following question, though, let him hold his breath. "Do you not wish to take off your cloak? Your gloves? It is warm."

She might have been right with the warmth, and the way she said it made him sure that she meant no harm, and he could not be upset at her for the question, but it… had surprised him.

"No. Forgive me, but I feel more comfortable this way." He answered hastily, and hoped it did not sound insulting nor unfriendly.

She gave him a look of understanding. He was relieved.

After a sip of her clear water (he wondered how the tavern keep had gotten clean water) she asked on, polite and friendly, and not curious in a bad way. "I am sure you have been to many places. Could you tell me of those? Also I wish to journey, but have no true destination yet."

He took a deep breath. Yes, he has seen so many places, yet he had never shared these memories. So he answered: "Places I have seen many, yet the end of my visit ended in the rarest cases in joy. I would not be able to give you something else besides my own bitter tales of each of those places. No, I doubt that that would help you."

But she did not give in, to his surprise. "Have you felt uncomfortable in every city, every forest, upon every mountain and every hill?"

No. But he could not tell her. He slowly wondered what she attempted to do…

"There were many places I had liked, yes, but even more so there were places which I learnt to despise, due to the creatures, mortal, fragile as they-" He stopped. He had said too much, and stood. He set down a few coins on the table, more than enough to pay for water and wine, then made his way outside, out of the tavern, just away. Away from these feelings, inherited from his father.

The Demon should never awaken in him.

Angel's Glory

here was once an angel. The angel was a proud one, his wings brilliant white and strong. He was loved and admired by all, but he was not happy. All loved and admired him, but no one did care for him. So he was a lonely angel. But he kept his smile, and he kept his gentle voice and his gentle touch.

As always, he flew the messages for his lord, for he was the swiftest of all on his wings. But for the first time, he came in to a storm he could not defeat. He was torn away by chilling winds, his feathers soaked and heavy by freezing rain, and lightning flashed to his left and right, threatening to strike him any moment. Then a final gust of wind and wet hit him. He was too exhausted to fight back. So without strength, he fell, deep and long, and far before he struck ground or sea, he lost consciousness.

As he woke up at last, he felt sore and chilled in every part of his body, down his very bones. That storm, he thought, was the most terrifying this world had ever seen. As he opened his eyes, thinking to find himself somewhere lost, or back home, he faced an unfamiliar pair of eyes, an unfamiliar smile, and an unfamiliar person.

"Where am I?" he asked, his voice quiet and broken, with no glimpse of its usual glory.

The stranger, like a mirror of his self, so he thought, finding those features as beautiful as his own, set a finger to his lips. "Speak not." The stranger said, and pulled back his finger and hand, moving on to change bandages that the angel only now noticed.

With surprise, he watched how his entire body was covered in bandages, and underneath, most surely, with wounds. He glanced to his wings, and he saw that they too had seen better days, all tattered and dirty, and nothing of their glory. And seeing his state, and seeing the area he was in – a mere bed, in a plain room with wooden walls – as well as seeing that he was treated by what seemed to be a mortal kin, he had to assume he was far off from home and his duties, and he feared, oh he feared, he would be lost in the mortal realm for a while. Despite his apparent savior's request, he began to speak again, with that soft, pale voice that was his this moment. "Who are you?" he wished to know. "Who are you, what are you, where am I, did you save me..." the stranger spoke. He seemed to know what the angel wanted to know. "I will tell you all, if you promise to spare your strength for your body to heal."

Seeing that he would receive all he wanted, he merely nodded, keeping his voice to himself this time. That made the stranger's smile only sweeter. "My name, my existence, is not of importance. Where we are I will tell you when your health allows you to continue your journey to whomever your message was thought for. No worries, I did not open it, and thus, neither did I read it. And if I am your savior? I would think so, yes, if picking you out of the stormy seas and bringing you here to mend you makes me a savior. I will keep you here only for as long as need be, knowing the tasks of your kind. Yes, I am very aware."

He was not sure how to deal with this, and it made him unsure of this stranger. It made him weary. But he was in no condition to do anything. He could not fly far, not in his state. And he was forbidden to ask, to speak. So he looked up to the plain ceiling, imagining a sky of stars as he would see in his home. With that, and his fatigue, he fell again in to a dark slumber. Days passed, days he could move and speak little. But he took the chances he received to speak and to move. His body ached with every inch he moved, but he did so anyway. And his voice pained as he tried to use it, but he used it anyway. He figured that his stranger was lonesome, and lived here, in this place. He figured that this stranger was far away from any other life besides the occasional animal. And he figured that this stranger knew very much about the immortal, far too much to be a mortal kin. Still, though, he found no name, no age, no heritage.

And so the days passed, speaking, moving more, chatting, walking finally, and him returning to his final glory again, his wings a brilliant white, his body relieved of all wounds and pain. "I thank you for the care, lonesome one, and I will never forget what I have received."

The man smiled only, and just before he wanted to leave, he was reminded of himself. Before he would say something though, the man spoke first. "I did all I could to give you the care you needed, 'lonesome one'. And if you need more mending, I will wait here. If you ever are broken by a storm again, come to me, and if you cannot, I will find you again. If you are ever in need of aid, ask me, I will aid you as good as I can. But most of all, do not smile that way to me if you do not mean it. Do not speak that way to me if you do not mean it. You have told me all of yourself while broken. You weeped all sorrow, and you cursed all fear. If admitted or not, you had been burdened dearly. But I was there to relieve you. So come to me if you are lonely."

With a true smile, a shy, unsure, but glad one, he nodded, and bowed his most courteous bow, showing his respect as well as gratitude. So he turned away, left that house in midst of grass and plains, and lifted himself again in to the skies, across wild seas and beautiful lands.

Having seen the most dreaded of storms, he also found the most beautiful care, and he knew, he would never again be lonely.

Far, far later, countless days past, he heard a tale of a lonesome angel. He had been the most glorious of all, but he had faded in his loneliness and left forever, to never return again to the world of the immortal. But he knew that that lonesome angel was no longer an angel, yet also no longer alone. And he knew, that the lonesome angel would never again return to the world of immortal, but would now always stay in touch with it.
So he smiled at the tale, with his full glory, wings of brilliant white and loved by all, knowing that since he had been broken, he would never again be lonely, and would never again lose his glory.